Groundwood Books / Douglas & McIntyre
720 Bathurst Street, Suite 500, Toronto, Ontario
M5S 2R4

Distributed in the USA by Publishers Group West
1700 Fourth Street, Berkeley, CA 94710

National Library of Canada Cataloguing in Publication
Argueta, Jorge
Trees are hanging from the sky / Jorge Argueta ;
illustrated by Rafael Yockteng; translated by
Elisa Amado.
Translation of: Los arboles estan colgando del cielo.
ISBN 0-88899-509-1
I. Yockteng, Rafael II. Amado, Elisa III. Title
PZ7.A73Tr 2003   j861'.64   C2002-904616-5

Library of Congress Control Number: 2002113187

Design by Michael Solomon
The illustrations are done in watercolor.
Printed and bound in China

For Luna Argueta and
Pablo Calderaro, who are always in
my dreams, and for Teresa Kennett
who makes them real…

J A

For Gabriela

RY

TREES ARE HANGING FROM THE SKY

WORDS BY JORGE ARGUETA   PICTURES BY RAFAEL YOCKTENG

GROUNDWOOD BOOKS DOUGLAS & McINTYRE TORONTO VANCOUVER BERKELEY

I see trees
hanging from
the sky.

Their roots are snakes
that in the day wind
around the clouds
so as not to fall.

I see trees
hanging from
the sky.

Pink trees.
Their branches are rivers
whooshing down
from high to low.

I see trees
hanging from
the sky.

Their leaves are fish,
crazy children
who fly and play
among the branches.

I see trees
hanging from
the sky.

At night
their roots are snakes
that wind tightly
around the stars
so as not to fall.

My mother sure
told me...

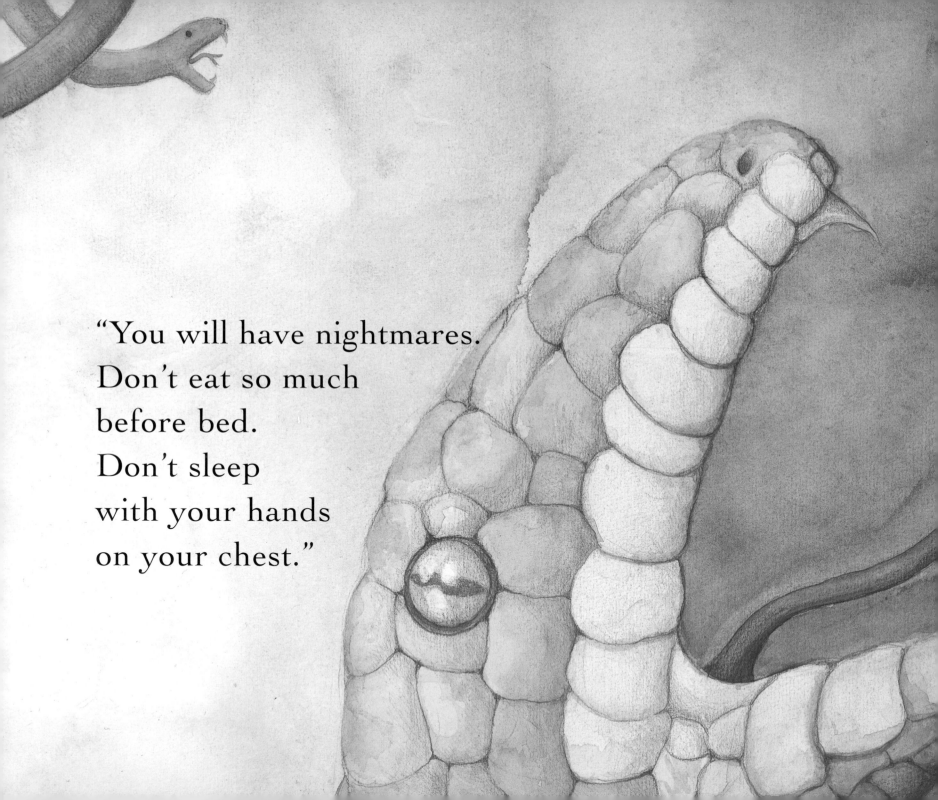

"You will have nightmares.
Don't eat so much
before bed.
Don't sleep
with your hands
on your chest."

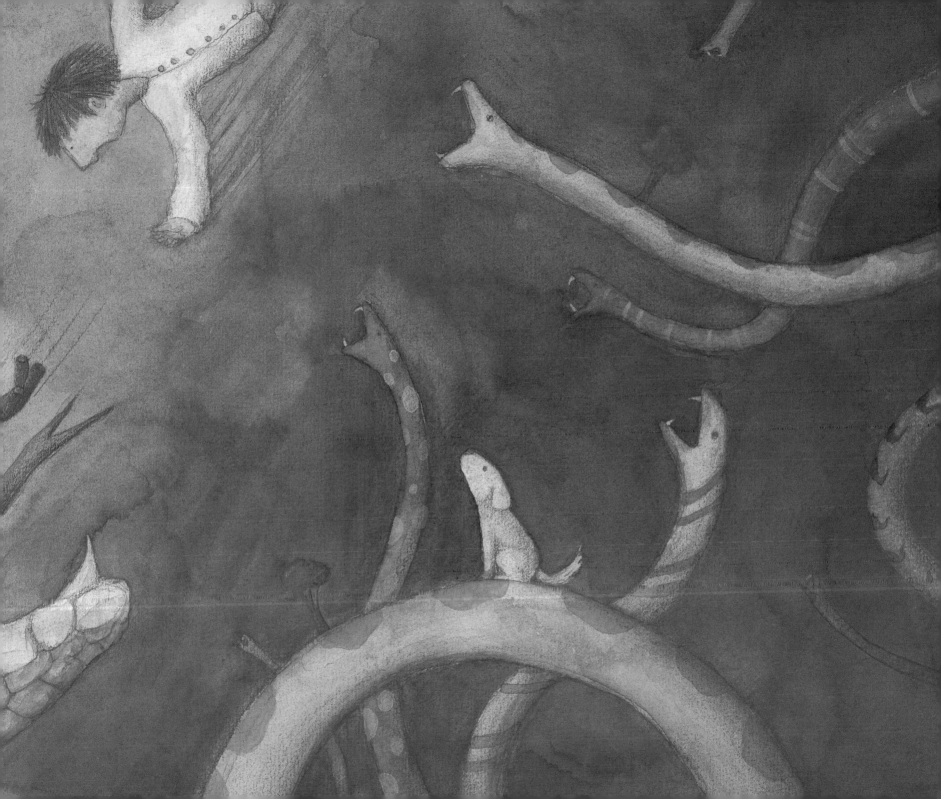

But seeing as how
I'm as stubborn
as a donkey,
here I am
seeing trees
hanging from
the sky.

I love
these pink trees
hanging head down
from the sky.

I love
their streams,
their snakes,
and their fish.
I love
their clouds
and their stars.

I want to dream like this
every night —
of pink trees
hanging head down
from the sky.

It's true
I'm scared of heights.
That's why my bed
is nice and low.
If my dreams make me fall
it won't hurt so much
when I hit the ground.